Jay Horne's

A LOUSY BEDTIME STORY

PRESENTED BY BOOKFLURRY INC.

Cover created by the author in Gimp assisted by Dall-e

Cataloguing Publication Data

Horne, Jay M., 1980-

Bookflurry Inc.

Bradenton, FL

TABLE OF CONTENTS

Introduction: Fleas and Gods

Once, there were many people who believed that the best way to keep the gods away was by praising them.

In actuality, a better way was to simply keep your area neat and tidy.

This is only natural since gods only seem to come along when something needs fixing. They just love to show their power by cleaning up a good mess.

If you don't believe me, just ask your children. They will tell you that a messy bedroom is sure to bring along Mom or Dad real soon.

And this is exactly as it should be, because the younger and smaller the creature, the more likely they will need the gods watching over them.

Of all the smallest creatures, Roland is the smartest. No one has to clean up after Roland. The gods wish everyone were more like him. But they also aren't the ones who have to smell Roland, or else they may reconsider.

Roland is a dung beetle. Look there he is now, pushing his little ball of poo up the hill toward his home. Sweat from a hard day's work collecting on his brow. Yes, there's nothing quite like a man who picks up after himself.

Instead, small gods are always on the lookout for people more like King Fleo. Fleo keeps the gods away by another tactic altogether. He tries to outrun them.

Being the King of a certain flock of lice comes with some responsibility. He ensures the flock's safety by keeping them on the move. As long as they are on a nice fresh patch of land, all things seem well. But sit for too long and the pudgy fingers of some small god come along and all you can do is pray. But, by that time praying sounds more like, "No. No. Please don't pluck us off and flush us down that swirly hole thingy!" rather than the nice bedtime prayers we so enjoy.

If he were smart like Roland, King Fleo would have learned to keep his area clean after that mess he'd left back on the land of Cutie Pie. Now, Fleo lives on Sherman the sheep and may just be the only living Sherminian to have ever seen a small god. That's how he knew there would be fingers.

King Fleo had so far been very lucky. It's not often you run from your problems and end up becoming the king of a nation. There is an old saying that goes, 'If you're not smart, you best be lucky' or something like that.

As luck would have it, Fleo had landed in his position after performing a leap of faith as fingers teased their way toward him with comb and pick. After that close brush with the gods (some gods prefer a brush to a comb) he began leading his new entourage in a never-ending march. Mostly because being the leader came with its advantages. Largely to do with another old saying that he had heard somewhere that goes something like this, 'you don't have to outrun the gods, you just have to outrun your friends'.

It's almost time to get on the move again. If you let lice sit around too long, things start to accumulate. When lice stop moving, they start eating, and anytime food is getting stuffed into one end of a louse there is bound to be something eventually coming out of the other.

Just look in any history book and you will see that when armies of anything cross over land of any sort they do something called laying waste. An army of lice does the exact same thing. In fact, Fleo's army had laid waste to the entire land from Sherman's neck to his little bobtail, and the waste they leave behind is the path that the small gods follow as they clean up their messes in their jolly sort of way. This is how they found Fleo before, but as we've said, Fleo isn't as smart as Roland, he's just lucky.

The thing about luck is, it tends to run out.

Chapter One: Good King Fleo

King Fleo thinks he is larger than life. Sherman would disagree if he were part of the argument. But Sherman wasn't a part of the argument, though the argument was happening just a few inches away from Sherman's ear.

Fleo glared down into the trough of one of the folds in Sherman's neck where the rest of his subjects had congregated. At least *they* weren't giving him any trouble. In fact, most of the village had their heads buried in the ground; he thought a rather smart way to avoid a king's scorn. But really, they were just hungry.

"I say, I say. don't shake your head at me, lad." The King demanded of the villager at hand.

The quiet villager shook in the gentle breeze clinging to a follicle of the King's good country with all its might.

King Fleo continued to search his pockets for his spectacles. "I do say, Sir, come a bit closer so I can see you clearly. Now, I say, there's still plenty of good ground to be worked. Yes, the follice is growing thicker each day, but you know what we've always said about too many follicles..."

Down in the trough, Grue, Milton, and Dilbert all plucked their heads from the soil and glanced up to where the King was defending his latest decision to march them up through the valley.

"Uh, what's does we say about there's bein' too any follicles, Dilbert?" asked Grue.

Dilbert looked puzzled, "Not any saying about there being too many follicles that I recall."

Then Milton said, "I reckon that may be because there ain't never been too many follicles afore. Am I right Dilbert?"

"How should I know?" said Dilbert. "Perhaps we should listen to what the king has to say about it."

"That's a good idea, Dilbert." Milton said, watching as the king really got to pointing his scepter at the fuzzy object wavering in the breeze.

"Uh, Dilbert?" asked Milton.

"Yes, Milton?"

"What do you suppose that dust mote's done to get the king in such a sore way, anywhos?"

"Not sure. But, whatever it was, he's really lettin' him have it."

Right about when King Fleo was explaining that if there wasn't a saying about too many follicles, that there shoulda been, the innocent fuzz ball broke free from its hold on the tree and crawled its way on the wind right toward the king in a rather lumbering but personally threatening manner.

King Fleo took cover under two of his four arms as it fluffed harmlessly by. He got hold of his bifocals just as the mote got itself snagged up further into the canopy like moss in a crowded woodland.

Grue chuckled through one large tooth. "Pfft ha ha pff."

"I say," said the King as he finally saw clearly, "isn't it a bit early for the fleece to be falling?" He quickly looked around in hopes no one caught him talking to the local fuzz. Of course, the congregation below had been one big blur till then.

"I say," mocked Dilbert, "Kingsy, what *was* that saying about too many follicles anyway?" The trio of insects laughed, causing the company of lice to turn from their meals.

King Fleo straightened his spectacles.

"It's said, I'm sure it's said, rather, land with strong hair, has the strongest roots." He put his four hands on his hips and nodded proudly at his tact.

King Fleo sometimes regretted his move from the darker forest of Cutie Pie, which occurred in one giant leap of faith on a crisp winter morning. The local Shermans only followed Fleo because, well, he was the one who always spoke up. Which tends to come with being the resident who finds the most to complain about. The constant Baaaaing and bleeeeting, mostly. But also, the frigid climate that just never seemed to let up. And the follicle forest here was simply too itchy to make any real outerwear from. Wool, they called it.

These were small misfortunes as compared to Cutie Pie's hostile terrain. But Fleo wouldn't mention that to the lice who looked up to him. Back on Pie, too many fleas in one section of land, and the big pinch just might come through and shear off ten or twenty comrades in a single go. Fleo once lost three friends who had bedded down in the northeastern ridge after being warned not to go near any caves.

Of course, caves and crevices aren't ideal hiding spots for fleas.

Carbon dioxide poisoning wouldn't be a known threat to fleas themselves. They just assumed settling in dark hairy interiors eventually made their comrades loopy, and then dead.

Cutie Pie, the dog, knew nothing of carbon dioxide poisoning either. She just knew when it was a good time to scratch behind her ear or nibble on her bum. And oh, how that made her feel much better. Otherwise, she was a professional sheep dog. Her master went in for all of that higher-thinking business, but being a tiny tale, our relevant characters do all of their thinking a bit lower to the ground.

It wasn't necessarily that Fleo thought he was larger than all of life, he just thought he was larger than all of lice. And to be fair, as far as size was concerned, he did have a head and shoulders on the rest. That, and he could jump. Yet jumping wasn't something he did often. His last jump had been scary enough. Once you break the canopy, all bets are off. The wind is unforgiving, and the whole world becomes entirely disorienting. Besides, if his followers found out that he had, well, fleed, for lack of a better word, from Cutie Pie to Sherman, the jokes would be relentless. And Fleo didn't do jokes.

Jokes, however, did do King Fleo because King Fleo had a rather big bottom, even for a Flea. The constant fun at his expense was what eventually made him decide to bounce. Here, Fleo got the respect he deserved. Of course, at first, there were a few lice who'd dared to comment on Fleo's large behind, but, they had quickly changed their tunes when Fleo threw his weight around a little.

It was easy to miss a tiny louse when the King needed somewhere to sit. In those instances, the louse's tune went from a normal baseline tenor to a high-pitched soprano. And then into a guffaw, before Fleo acknowledge his lumpy perch. If the King did do Jokes, he may have made one about their sounding rather flat.

He had to admit, lice could carry a decent tune when they wanted. There wasn't anything quite like a procession of parasites clicking claws to the rhythm of bah bah black sheep. It sounded much like Marvin used to when he was practicing his tap-dancing routine. Marvin had also bounced from Cutie Pie, though his was in a blind effort to join the circus.

Now, there was a rolling murmur among the king's throng. He, at least, had kept a little embarrassment at bay. Best to get moving while he had their attention. Fleo placed his barbed leg across his left two hands and with the hair of his right forearm began to play.

With only a few objections, the procession began filing up the hill toward the king, clapping their claws to the beat of Fleo's parade march.

Once they got moving, these lice really were a force to be

reckoned with. If they kept up this pace, they'd be on the shadowy side before the rain came.

Dilbert was trying not to laugh at one of Grue's latest remarks when he noticed the King looking their way. Quietly they ambled along behind the King's bottom which had begun bobbing to the rhythm.

Chapter Two: A Regal Rendezvous

The stately procession of King Fleo's flock marched on, claws clacking merrily to his pompous marching tune. As they crested a plateau of pebbled skin behind Sherman's ear, a startling sight gave them pause - another royal parade approaching from the opposite rise!

At its head marched a slender white louse bedecked in fuzzy finery. She had a regal bearing, but stood no taller than a single thick bristle. Behind wafted a banner woven from fine downy hairs, a masterpiece painted in vivid grease-bound pigments depicting the apparent queen lined with ermine mantling.

The two leaders eyed each other in surprise as their followers spilled onto the plateau. Murmurs rippled through the crowd.

"Well, seems we have a welcoming party for my arrival into these parts," proclaimed King Fleo loudly, unwilling to be outdone even in apparent hospitality.

Grue laughed belligerently, elbowing Milton which drew awkward stares from the collective audience. Dilbert put a hand over Grue's mouth when the Queen's eyes lit on the trio.

"Rather presumptuous for a fat flea to style himself king in my domain," said the Queen in cool tones, slowly looking Fleo up and down.

Her following cheered, "Queen Clouse's domain!"

From behind King Fleo Milton declared, "You go get her Kingsy!" and a weak rattle of laughter came from the Queen's company.

King Fleo puffed up his chest and adjusted his glasses. "We can do better than that lads! Let's have a cheer!"

From down in front came Grue among the silence, "Uh. Is this havin' to do with the follicles, Dilbert?"

Again the Queen's company laughed.

"Now see here, I shall have you know that I am exploring new lands in which to found the Grand Flea Empire, soon to stretch from flank to withers!" blustered King Fleo.

"Is that so? And I suppose our Peaceable Queendom of Utopian Lice shall simply scurry out of your way?" riposted Clouse, eyes narrowing.

King Fleo raised his scepter and shouted, "Men!"

Queen Clouse raised her scepter and the claws of her army began to click in anticipation.

Fleo shouted, "At the ready!"

Then, suddenly the Queen burst into peals of laughter, dissolving the King's serious look into one of question.

The Queen could hardly catch her breath! Her laugh was so funny King Fleo could hardly keep from cracking a smile of his own.

When the Queen finally got a breath she put a hand on Fleo's shoulder and pointed past him. "Just look!"

He turned and saw his entire company had their heads stuck deep in the ground.

Fleo could no longer contain himself. He burst into laughter and the Queen and her entourage joined in.

Eventually, Grue, Dilbert, and Milton plucked their heads out to see what was all the commotion.

"No more knuckle sandwiches then, Dilbert?"

"I think it's safe 'um," said Milton.

The laughter caught with them as well and soon Fleo's whole entourage had their heads up and were laughing along.

When the laughter finally faded, King Fleo and Queen Clouse looked at one another seriously.

Then from behind King Fleo Grue said, "Uh, Dilbert?"

"Yes, Grue."

"What's was'n we's a laughin's for all dat then?"

And the King and Queen burst out laughing all over again.

Fleo timed a lull, made a flourish of his ermine cape, and said more jovially, "We may have more to gain from an allegiance than petty quibbling methinks. Let us dine together Your Highness and see what our fair courts may achieve united."

"Indeed, I should be delighted!" smiled Clouse, curtsying gracefully as her lice again erupted in cheers for the clever compromise.

And so beneath the glow of a golden hour upon Sherman's leathery horizon, the two monarchs held court together. Amidst friendly banter, they soon perceived a natural chemistry between their leadership styles, and perhaps soon after that, a more personal fondness blossomed as well. Where that may lead none could yet say. But the realm seemed brighter while they all dined together.

Jay Horne

Chapter Three: Fleeing the Gods

It's been some time since we've checked on our old friend Roland the dung beetle. The small gods, fickle as they are, still tend to look kindly on Roland. There he is now, sleeping soundly in his bed; his ball of poo resting neatly in the corner ready to be rolled along the following morning.

The same could not be said for our careless colony.

The unified flea and louse processions marched onward, voices raised in song under the mingled banners of King and Queen. Through sheer force of numbers, they carved a winding path along the commanding topography of Sherman's hide.

What the parading parasites failed to consider was the environmental impact imparted by their tiny footsteps. As evident by the trails of debris, discarded shells, and micro droppings left in their wake…not to mention a faint smell to the air.

Excrement is something always in sure supply. Luck however, has its limits. And theirs, was about to run out.

The party alighted upon a sheer ivory cliff face. Queen Clouse and King Fleo looked out through the fleece mesh at a shifting dark sky.

"That's my homeland passing near," said Fleo.

It gave him a sudden pang of worry. Memories of life back on Pie came flooding back.

"This cliff may take a bit of time to navigate with this large company. Let's let them rest and you can tell me about it," said the Queen.

Fleo looked back nervously at the trail of litter coming down the hill. The party had already started poking their heads into the soil. "My dear Clouse, I must warn you— I have run into this problem before."

"Whatever do you mean?" inquired Clouse with a furrowed brow.

"I don't think it's wise to stop."

Just then came a tremor through the continent of Sherman.

"I fear the small gods may be upon us. Once I saw many of my fleas wiped out by the terrible Snip for irritating the gods with our brazen feats of mountain climbing in the Schnauz."

"My word, how dreadful!" Clouse brought a spindly foreleg to her mouth. "But whatever can we do?"

A terrible shadow passed overhead and Fleo's face went grim.

"Run!"

For it was none other than the gods themselves come to harvest Sherman's wool! Colossal hands and fingers hovered above them; great blades of silver snipping in their grips.

In the initial moments of chaos there issued terrified screams and lamentations. But Fleo called to Clouse and together they corralled their subjects.

"Make haste away! Follow us!"

Holding banners bravely aloft they led the lice in rapid retreat just as giant shears crashed deafeningly behind. The musical parade beat a hasty rhythm of escape, racing the gods' terrible clippings as tufts of fleece avalanched behind them.

As the valley narrowed dangerously, King Fleo spied a daring route of escape - a lone errant strand of long uncut wool poking from the sheep's bare skin, and there across a great divide was Cutie Pie, stalking hungrily nearby. Mind racing, Fleo hastily took his crimson banner as the thundering gods closed in all around them.

"You'll not leave us?" cried Queen.

"I shall secure a lifeline to the far side! Stand ready to follow my lead!" he bellowed. With knees bent and banner streaming, noble Fleo gathered his full courage and launched out into the void!

The icy teeth of death nipped at his heels as Fleo flew recklessly through empty space.

But alas the gods favored his boldness this day!

His barbed grip caught firm hold of Cutie Pie's fur tufts and the world spun dizzyingly around him.

Heart throbbing against his exoskeleton, Fleo looped the wool strand around an exposed root. "That... should... do it."

Back across the divide, on a naked stretch of land, Fleo's subjects whimpered in despair. But then they saw it. The King's rippling banner was waving out in the dark.

"There!" called Queen Clouse and she tightened the wool. "It's sturdy!"

Some of the subjects shared worried looks as they formed a line.

"It's time we move onto new lands. It's good strong wool. Just don't look down," called the Queen.

One by one, encouraged by their Queen's gentle nod, they stepped onto the narrow rope bridge.

Dilbert and his posse were the last to dare the pass. He stopped beside the Queen and she nodded encouragingly. "Ladies first my Queen."

She smiled, but before she could make a move, Grue came ploughing through. "No askin' twice, Dilbert. Me's a lady."

Then Milton ran across after, trying to educate Grue on the differences between boys and girls.

They both laughed. Then the Queen and Dilbert started across to the strange new world.

Chapter Four: Seeking Shelter

Having narrowly dodged doom, the worn-out group of lice clung tightly to their new home in Cutie Pie's shaggy coat. But even as they caught their breath, new dangers set in. The dog's scratching was going to make it a dangerous jog to relative safety.

"We best skedaddle!" hollered King Fleo.

"On two?" asked the Queen, lifting her foreleg, and preparing to strum.

Fleo paused. Took in the full sight of her, and smiled. Then he prepared his own musical limb.

To the sound of the old parade march, messy rows formed behind their tattered banners and the bone-tired refugees marched swiftly over the vibrating land and under the constant shifting shadows of Cutie's scratching paw.

"It's a bit more shadowy here on Pie, but when the sky breaks through, it sure is beautiful," said the King to Queen Clouse, reckoning the coast clear for now.

As the sky darkened to a crisp country night, Fleo and Clouse leaned cozy against one other. Serious notions of starting over flickered hopefully in their minds.

Fleo dared to take Clouse's slender claw, "A fair bit of life yet awaits if'n we work as one." He gave her claw an affectionate squeeze.

Just then three familiar raspy laughs echoed from the scrubby brush. Why, it was Grue, Milton, and Dilbert emerging raggedy but smiling!

"Well, looks like this here royal duo figured out they make quite the pair!" said Dilbert.

Milton elbowed Grue. "Reckon they gonna rule as queen and…king-consort now?"

Grue scratched his head. "Consort? You mean like one's them there musical bands?"

Dilbert butted in snickering, "Naw you goob, he's pokin' at how Mr. Fleo be twice the size of little lady Clouse!"

"Mostly in the britches!" said Milton.

All three rustics fell into knee-slapping guffaws.

The jokes didn't faze King Fleo one bit. In fact, he put his glasses on just to see the goofballs rallying together and it filled his heart near to bursting.

Besides, he wasn't running from insults about his weight, ever again.

Then something strange happened. Dilbert said, "Without legs like those, he'd have never made that jump."

Milton looked struck with sobriety. "Guess, you're right, Dilbert."

Grue said, "Uh, Milton?"

"Yes, Grue?"

Then he pointed to each of them individually, starting with himself. "I thought I was on the right. You see. I is standing here. That'd makes you middle. Cuz, you's standing about there, 'tween us. And Dilbert woulds be…"

Milton threw his hands in the air. "Alright! Alright!"

"No's. Not alls threes of us can be. Just me's a being on da right."

The Queen and King smiled at one another.

Jay Horne

Chapter Five: An Unexpected Reunion

King Fleo was awoken by a faint sound on the wind. He stood up and lost ear of it for a second. But then, there it was again. The pitter-patter of tiny feet tap dancing out a snappy rhythm! Could it be...?

He woke the Queen and dragged her to the hilltop in the dark. They peered out from Cutie Pie's furry mane and beheld an astonishing sight. There under the twinkling stars stood a makeshift circus tent cobbled together from bits of wool, moss, and who knows what. Cavorting about the ring was none other than Fleo's old friend Marvin, clad in a sequined vest and miniature top hat! The eccentric flea was tapping up a veritable storm, teaching new steps to his troupe of performing mites.

"Well tickle me pink!" exclaimed King Fleo in happy surprise. He gave a loud whistle back to the snoozing company who started to stir. Then he waved, catching Marvin's eye.

With an excited gasp, the exuberant entertainer came bounding over to embrace his long-lost friend.

After a flurry of excited backslapping and antennae

fluttering in greeting, Marvin excitedly offered the road-weary party prime seating at his show.

They all settled in. Fleo felt his spirit lift watching Marvin dance with such joy, his troupe's antics coaxing first giggles, then outright guffaws from the audience.

With the show at an end and morale greatly improved, the groups dined together.

"Oh, I've always wanted to join a traveling show," said Queen Clouse to Fleo.

"Oh," interrupted Marvin. "This is no traveling show."

Fleo and Clouse looked at one another nervously.

"But, how do you avoid the…" Fleo gulped. "The you know what?"

"Well, you know our balancing act. The chap you seen walkin' on top of that ball?"

"Yeah."

"Well, I picked that act up from a beetle down on good Mother Earth. Good guy. Names Roland."

The fleas at the dinner table all started nodding feverishly.

"Anyhow," said Marvin, more than the act even, he taught me something else important."

Fleo and Clouse were rapt.

"Cleanliness, my friends, is godliness." Marvin picked up a sweet piece of candied Cutie and popped it in his mouth. "That's why we clean up after every show."

Queen Clouse sat back in her chair, the color draining from her pink cheeks. "You mean, you help them?"

"Absolutely Queensy! It's the ants and bees that go in for all that higher up stuff and they're always angry."

Fleo and Clouse looked at one another nervously.

Marvin burst out laughing. "I'm just pokin' fun at you two! You're gonna love it here. Because we have another thing… Life-changing, I tell ya."

Marvin came over and put an arm around each of their shoulders. "It's called a toilet."

"A toil it?" said Fleo.

"That's right. A toilet. Yes, my friends. It is indeed a whole new world."

Epilogue

While the fleas and louse dare to envision a tidier empire, Cutie Pie the collie settles onto her haunches, doing her best to ignore the traveling itch that has just moved over her shoulders and a bit down her back.

Sherman the sheep resumes placidly grazing, blissfully unruffled by his shearing, but still just as likely to disagree.

And the towering human masters? Why, they gather up bundles of shorn fleece and amble off with not a thought for the tiny world and mighty kingdoms that flit and crawl through the hairy jungles which cling to their pets and livestock.

Don't feel bad for Cutie Pie, the gods who go in for all that higher-thinking stuff tend to scratch her accordingly. Besides, the more interesting stories always seem to occur a bit closer to the ground.

THE END

OTHER BOOKS BY JAY HORNE

When Doctor Shandler genetically engineers a rapid-growing breed of caimans at Tampa's Lowry Park Zoo, his experiment spirals out of control, threatening bystanders and staff alike.

Evoking the science fantasy vision of Michael Crichton's Jurassic Park and Congo, the unintended reptilian beasts unleash chaos amidst hurricane Zolo until compassion prevails from unlikely heroes. Can the mutant outbreak be reversed before the zoo lies in ruins?

Science Fiction/Genetic Engineering/40 Minute Read

Doctor Datson is getting older, but that doesn't keep him from still getting into mischief.
When one of his lab experiments re-animates some fossils, it is up to Truman and rest of the gang to track down dangerous creatures and find who's responsible.
Minute Flash Fiction
Science Fiction/Thriller/Humor

old
the
the
out
30

Chilling tales blend nostalgic Americana backdrops with doses of creepy whimsy à la Ray Bradbury. Wickedly humorous at times, make no mistake – malice lurks behind the smirks. Like classic Twilight Zone, these stories shock more than they soothe.

The Death of Science is a twisted and humorous foray into the vast multi-faceted universe of Rootworld. Like a contemporary Twilight Zone, this satirical science fiction fantasy tale will appeal to fans of both the nostalgic familiar as well as the shockingly bizarre.

A Lousy Bedtime Story

For free goodies, join our newsletter at

bookflurry.substack.com